08/23

Harmony's Journey

7

HarperCollins®, ☰®, and Harper Festival® are trademarks of HarperCollins Publishers.

Bella Sara: Harmony's Journey
Cover and interior illustrations by Spoops
Copyright © 2009 Hidden City Games, Inc. © 2005–2009 conceptcard. All rights reserved.
BELLA SARA is a trademark of conceptcard and is used by Hidden City Games under license.
Licensed by Granada Ventures Limited.
Printed in the United States of America.
No part of this book may be used or reproduced in any manner whatsoever without written
permission except in the case of brief quotations embodied in critical articles and reviews. For
information address HarperCollins Children's Books, a division of HarperCollins Publishers,
10 East 53rd Street, New York, NY 10022.
www.harpercollinschildrens.com
www.bellasara.com

Library of Congress catalog card number: 2008942551
ISBN 978-0-06-168786-0
09 10 11 12 13 CG/CW 10 9 8 7 6 5 4 3 2
❖
First Edition

Harmony's Journey

Written by Felicity Brown
Illustrated by Spoops

HarperFestival®
A Division of HarperCollins Publishers

1

"My name is Lorelei Stemmel," Lorelei chanted. "I'm twelve years old. I live . . . I live . . ."

Her words trailed off and tears came to her eyes. That was all she knew—her name and age. And that she was frightened.

Lorelei shivered and wrapped her arms around herself as a cool night breeze whispered through the leaves. The dark forest surrounded her, its looming trees and choking vines cutting off all but the barest whisper of midsummer moonlight from overhead. Where was she? How had she gotten here? Why couldn't she remember anything that had happened more than five minutes ago? She closed her eyes and strained her mind. All she could dredge up was the image of a sad-eyed young girl with reddish-brown curls along with a few notes of faraway music, wistful and faint. . . .

Caw!

Lorelei's eyes flew open. An enormous bird, sulfur-yellow with red eyes, was diving directly at her. Its cruel, curved black beak gaped open in a cry of triumph.

"No!" Lorelei cried, spinning and pushing her way through the tangle of underbrush. Brambles tore at her clothes and her long brown hair as she ran. Still she could hear the caw of the nightmarish bird. She caught a glimpse of it flapping overhead as she ran. The crow was larger than any bird she'd ever seen.

There's no such thing as a giant yellow crow, Lorelei told herself. *This must be nothing but a bad dream. Why won't I wake up?*

"Ow!" she shrieked, as she bumped her head on a massive, gnarled branch hanging low over the trail. She staggered to a stop, stunned for a moment by the impact.

The crow dived toward the spot where she was standing. Only the selfsame branch stopped its razor-tipped talons from reaching their mark.

"What do you want?" she shouted, as she dived between two massive tree trunks. "Why are you chasing me?"

The crow let out another shrill caw, diving down and cutting off that line of escape. Lorelei was forced to turn back, dodging around the trees and back into the underbrush.

I can't let it catch me, she thought, wincing as a tangleberry thorn caught the bare skin of her arm. *If I do, Serena will . . . What?*

Her thoughts paused at the name: Serena. Once again the image of that curly-haired girl swam into view out of the blankness of her memory. Serena. Her . . .

sister? Yes! She remembered now. Serena was her younger sister. She was eight years old. She . . .

Yet another caw cut off her thoughts. Looking forward, Lorelei saw that the crow was blocking her path again just ahead. Veering off to the left, she followed a narrow trail that meandered among the trees. She guessed it must have been made by horses or some other hoofed creature.

I can't let it catch me, she thought, as she heard the crow shriek again. *I can't let it catch me.* The words matched the rhythm of her running feet and formed a frantic melody in her mind. *I can't let it catch me. I can't let it* . . .

She burst into a large, grassy meadow. Panic propelled her several yards into the open before she realized it. She stopped short, realizing she was now easy pickings for the crow.

She scanned the moonlit sky, backing slowly toward the shelter of the tree line. But to her amazement, there was neither

sign nor sound of the horrible yellow creature. She let out a cautious sigh of relief,
resting a hand against the rough bark of the
nearest tree. Then she jumped as something
hissed at her from the darkness. A slither-
ing sound told her she'd just disturbed some
unseen creature. True, the shadows of the
trees offered some shelter, she told herself as
she moved back into the open. But everyone
knew there was also much to fear within the
depths of Darkcomb Forest. . . .

Darkcomb Forest! she thought, once
again grasping at a familiar name. *Yes! That's
where I am. The deepest, most mysterious forest in North of North, that stretches from
Mount Whitemantle to the banks of Horseshoe
Bay. And my own home is . . . is . . .*

But it was no use. The memories
slipped out of reach as quickly as that slith-
ering nighttime creature. All she could hold
on to was the vague images of a dreary villa
of tumbledown stone, a stooped man with
burning dark eyes, and several blobs of colorful fuzz that bounded out of view before

6

she could remember what they were. And, of course, her sister's face. The look in Serena's sad eyes told her that returning soon was important; that something terrible would happen if she did not. But how could she help her sister if she couldn't even remember what was wrong?

Tears of frustration sprang to Lorelei's eyes. Her head hummed with the sense of her own helplessness . . . and, after a moment, with the faint strains of some unfamiliar melody, simple yet haunting.

For a second or two she thought the music was coming from within her own mind. After all, wasn't that how she always reacted in times of stress, sadness, or fear? By retreating into the safety and solace of music?

Wait, how did I know that? she thought. *Is it another memory?*

She wanted to stop and figure it out, but the music was winding its way into her, making it impossible to focus on anything else. Her shoulders started swaying to the rhythm, and her legs joined in, carrying her farther into the meadow. Her mouth opened of its own will, and she began to sing along in a soft but clear voice. She clamped her lips shut, not wanting to give herself away, but still she found herself humming along.

What if it's a trap? she thought. She almost turned back to the forest. But the melody was growing louder, tickling her somewhere behind the wall that was blocking most of her memories. At that moment, the moonlight caught the shape of a horse cresting a hillock. No, not a horse—a foal. It was a weanling filly, as slender and graceful as the finest Arabian, but with a shimmering coat of luminescent violet. Her dainty hooves and bushy mane and tail were silvery purple, and her large, intelligent eyes glowed like amethysts. Beside the filly, floating along in midair, was a sparkling golden lyre. Its gleaming strings trembled with each movement of the foal's head or hooves. Although Lorelei had never seen such a thing before, she understood without a doubt that the young horse was controlling the lyre and making the music that now filled the clearing.

Two more foals frolicked into view behind the first. One was ghostly white with ink-black eyes. Her tiny hooves barely seemed to touch the ground as she pranced to the music. The other was a unicorn, a jet-black colt with gossamer wings folded against his withers and a half grown silvery white horn sprouting from beneath his fuzzy forelock. He snorted and bucked as he danced along. Occasionally he sprang up and flapped his not-fully-grown wings to try to hold himself in the air for a few seconds before falling back to the ground with a frustrated snort. Behind the foals came a furry gray creature about the size of a large squirrel. He had conical ears and a long thin tail with a thick tip that struck the ground along with the rhythm of the lyre's song. *A tomtomme,* Lorelei realized, as another piece of her memory returned. *That's a tomtomme. There are lots of them living along the edges of the forest.*

She barely had time to savor this small victory over her lost memory before she realized she had started singing along with the violet filly's song once again. Her voice rose, mingling effortlessly with the melody.

The foals and their tomtomme friend heard her. Abruptly, the music stopped.

2

The black colt let out a snort of surprise and pawed the ground. The pale filly spooked and spun, running a few strides back the way she'd come. But the violet filly took a step forward, eyeing Lorelei curiously.

"Hello," Lorelei said, looking directly into the filly's amethyst eyes. "My name is Lorelei. I liked your song."

The filly merely stared for a long moment. Lorelei held her breath, not sure what would happen next.

Then the filly tossed her head, and

the floating lyre began to play again. The tomtomme scampered forward and began keeping time with his tail.

Lorelei began to hum along. Part of her wanted to fall into the music and never return. Hearing her voice mingling with the filly's lyre, she felt as if she'd finally found what she'd been seeking.

But another part struggled against the song, although she wasn't sure why. Suddenly, words flooded into her mind, matching the melody. She couldn't resist opening her mouth to sing:

> The lyrics seem to come to me,
> Just like a distant memory;
> I gladly sing the melody
> To add to your sweet harmony;
> To sing with you I must agree
> Our music is a jubilee,
> With each note played so carefully,
> The way sweet music ought to be;
> For I will sing the melody,
> And you will be my harmony.

As she sang, Lorelei drifted up the hillock to join the foals. The white filly had returned, and both she and the colt danced along with the music. From where she stood, Lorelei could see the whole of the meadow stretching before her. Grazing in the distance was a small herd of adult horses—these foals' parents, she guessed. A rose-pink unicorn and a proud, black, winged unicorn. A creamy white horse with blue beads in her mane and a black horse with a leopard-skin cape. A glistening lavender-maned mare and a golden stallion.

As the song ended, Lorelei found her gaze lingering on the peaceful herd. Seeing them there made her feel happy and sad at the same time. Horses were everywhere in North of North, of course, but Lorelei rarely had the chance to interact with them.

Really? she thought, catching herself. *Wait, how do I know that?*

Just then the lyre finished with a flourish, and the violet filly let out an approving neigh. The colt kicked up his heels with joy, and the pale foal perked her ears happily.

The musical filly took a step forward. Lorelei gasped as her mind suddenly flooded with vivid images. After the uncertainty of her memory loss, it was enough to make her knees buckle. She nearly fell to the ground. The filly jumped back, startled by the reaction, and the images suddenly blinked off.

"No!" Lorelei cried. "Please. It's all right. I was just—just surprised, that's all."

She realized now what had happened. Horses in North of North could communicate with humans by projecting images into their minds. Lorelei knew that such magic happened all the time. Even without most of her memories, however, she was quite certain this was the first time it had happened to her.

The filly lowered her head cautiously. The images came again, more slowly this time. Lorelei focused on the vision the filly was sending her: It was a slender, brown-haired girl. She gasped as she recognized . . . herself! She appeared to be singing, although no sound came from her mouth, only a stream of blue, like a beam of light. Then another stream appeared from some unseen singer, this one as green as a forest glade. The two streams joined and intertwined, forming a beautiful rainbow.

"I get it!" Lorelei blurted out. "Harmony! You're telling me your name is Harmony?"

The filly tossed her head, and the lyre emitted a string of sparkling notes. Lorelei grinned.

"Harmony," she repeated. "It's the perfect name."

The unicorn colt barged forward, snorting impatiently and pawing the ground. Lorelei smiled, guessing that he wanted to share his name next. Before long, they were all acquainted. The black colt was known as Dart. The pale filly was Moonsprite. Harmony even sent images into Lorelei's mind to introduce the tomtomme, whose name was Bongo.

"It's nice to meet you all," Lorelei

said. "I wonder if your parents would mind if I stayed with you for a while. You see, I seem to have forgotten . . . to have forgotten . . ."

Harmony tilted her head quizzically as the girl's words trailed off, but Lorelei hardly noticed. She'd just caught the faintest whisper of some distant melody, carried to her by the night breezes. The voice was beautiful, although plaintive and weak at the same time.

Lorelei gasped as more memories came flooding back. She'd heard that voice before, many times. "It's Serena!" she cried. Finally noticing the foals' curious stares, she tried to explain what she had just thought she had heard. It was difficult, though—she could hardly understand any of this herself. "My sister. I can hear her singing. I think— I think she's in trouble. I have to find her!"

She turned and rushed back the way she'd come. She'd hardly gone three steps when the pounding of small hooves surrounded her, nearly drowning out the faint sound of her sister's voice. The foals had caught up to her, Harmony in the lead.

"You believe me? Really?" Tears came to Lorelei's eyes as Harmony flooded her mind with more images. "And you'll come with me? Help me find her? Oh, thank you!" Then she hesitated, remembering the terrifying yellow crow. "But are you sure? It could be dangerous. Your parents . . ."

Dart snorted, rearing up defiantly. Harmony stamped one foot. Bongo smacked the ground firmly with his tail. Even Moonsprite cast only one nervous glance toward the distant herd before stepping forward. Despite her worry, Lorelei smiled faintly.

"All right," she said. "I suppose we'll be back before they notice. It isn't far."

She blinked, wondering how she knew that. But there was no time to waste on such thoughts. The foals were already trotting ahead toward the edge of the forest. Tilting her head to catch the faint sound of her sister's voice, Lorelei hurried after them.

* * *

Serena's song led Lorelei and her new friends toward the north. Somehow the path seemed much clearer this time, making Lorelei wonder how she'd ever become lost.

"I only hope that crow doesn't come back," she murmured, glancing upward. Seeing that the others were confused, she told them about being chased by the terrifying yellow bird.

While she was talking, her sister's song grew even fainter. Lorelei paused, straining to hear. But after a few more notes, the song died away completely.

Panic gripped her, making breathing hard. What if the song didn't return? She would be lost again, with no hope of ever finding her sister, or even escaping from this terrible forest. . . .

A chorus of notes surrounded her, calming her instantly. Sensing Lorelei's distress, Harmony was playing a few soothing chords.

As the lyre's music faded, Serena's returned. It was still faint, but perhaps a bit closer, giving Lorelei new hope.

"Come on," she said eagerly, turning down a fork in the trail. "I think she's this way!"

She broke into a jog. The foals trotted along behind her, with Bongo hitching a ride between Dart's wings. Serena's voice grew louder. They were almost there!

The sun was peeking over the horizon when they rounded a curve in the path and Lorelei saw the forest open up into a flat, rocky clearing surrounded by a tall, crumbling stone wall. A stone archway revealed a few pale buildings and an old fountain covered in a thick layer of dust and cobwebs. Weeds sprouted in the cobblestone courtyard, and thick grass grew knee-high everywhere else. The place had clearly been abandoned many years before.

Serena's voice had faded again, and Lorelei could feel Harmony trying to question her. Her thoughts were churning, her memory struggling against the thick fog that still held it captive.

"I-I think this is the place," she said uncertainly.

That seemed to be enough for Dart. He stepped toward the archway with the two fillies right behind him. All of them were eyeing the lush grass.

Lorelei opened her mouth. Something about this place seemed strangely familiar, and she was suddenly filled with dread. But before she could speak, her new friends had disappeared inside the wall.

When she followed, she saw that Dart and Moonsprite were already nibbling at the grass. Meanwhile, Harmony was watching as Bongo crouched over something on the ground, chittering curiously. Lorelei's worry increased as she hurried forward to see what he'd found.

It was a music box, an ornate wooden chest decorated with musical notes and symbols. She gasped as her memories came flooding back.

"Wait!" she cried, as Bongo reached for the music box's lid. "Noooo!"

In a flash of light, the scene around them changed: Where the buildings and wall had stood crumbling, they now appeared whole and new. The cobblestones gleamed amid manicured shrubs and trees. Festive lights hung over the square and crystal-clear water bubbled in the fountain.

"Welcome back, Lorelei," said a voice behind her.

She spun around to see a tall, thin, stooped man standing between her and the archway. He was wearing a long blue velvet cloak and a matching vest. Long white hair flowed out from under his silk top hat, and his bushy white eyebrows twitched with amusement.

The Maestro.

How could she ever have forgotten him—or what he'd done to her and her family? "Stay away from him!" she cried to her new friends. "He—"

Then the Maestro pulled a conductor's baton from his cloak and pointed it at her. Immediately, Lorelei's words were frozen in her throat. Lorelei glared at him helplessly, knowing better than to struggle against the baton's power.

The Maestro strolled toward Harmony, still keeping his baton trained on Lorelei. The foals were exchanging confused glances, but Harmony stood bravely as the man looked her over, paying special attention to the lyre floating beside her.

"What a lovely instrument," he commented.

Bongo had leaped up onto Dart's back again at the man's first appearance. Now he chittered nervously, banging his tail against the colt's side.

"Aha!" The Maestro sounded pleased. "And a tomtomme. Excellent! How about a little song, shall we?"

Lorelei quivered with rage. She couldn't believe he'd done it again. But she was helpless to resist the magic of his baton when he flicked his wrist in her direction. Her mouth opened of its own accord, and her voice poured out, pure and strong.

Then the Maestro pointed the baton at Bongo and Harmony. The little tom-tomme jumped down from Dart's back and began to pound his tail rhythmically against the ground. Notes poured from Harmony's lyre, joining in with Lorelei's song.

Moonsprite began to dance. Even Dart swayed back and forth.

As the song rose to a crescendo, the Maestro laughed with delight. "Excellent!" he cried. "You've done well this time, Lorelei."

He lowered the baton, and the spell was broken. Dart snorted in dismay and backed away. Moonsprite and Bongo looked confused. Harmony turned to stare at Lorelei, a question in her amethyst eyes.

"I'm sorry," Lorelei whispered.

The Maestro grabbed her arm and yanked her to him, aiming the baton at her so that her tongue froze again. "No need for apologies. You only did as I ordered— sought some suitable new musicians to add to my collection." He surveyed the others. "I have no use for a dancing filly or a half-pint unicorn. But a foal with a magical lyre will do nicely. And the tomtommé, too!"

3

Dart and Moonsprite trumpeted in alarm. Harmony spun and tried to gallop away. But the Maestro raised his baton, stopping the violet foal in her tracks.

"Let's not panic, my friends," he said, reaching for a monocle hanging from his vest. Lorelei winced when she saw it. The baton was bad enough—it controlled others' bodies. But the monocle was even worse. With that, the Maestro could control their minds.

Now that Lorelei's memories were back, she almost wished they weren't. Using both magical objects together was how the Maestro made his living. After Serena and Lorelei's parents had died in a fire, the Maestro had taken the sisters under his wing. He made them travel all over North of North and forced them to put on musical shows in towns and hamlets from Reinshead to the Jasmine Forest for weeks on end without rest. And now he was planning to add Harmony and Bongo to his show! How could she have done this to them?

"Come, my lovely," the Maestro was cooing at Harmony. He held the monocle to his eye. Its lens swirled with cloudy colors. "There's no need to be alarmed."

Harmony trembled. So did the strings of her lyre. An uncertain jumble of notes poured forth. Then she seemed to relax.

"I'm your friend," the Maestro continued, his monocle still trained on the violet foal.

Harmony stepped forward. Stretching her neck out, she softly nuzzled the man's hand. Lorelei knew exactly how the foal must be feeling. Under the power of the monocle, everything the man said *felt* as if it were completely true and real. Harmony was helpless to resist, just as Lorelei herself had been many, many times.

"That's better." The Maestro glanced around. All three foals were gazing at him placidly. So was Bongo. Only Lorelei seemed to be still in possession of her real feelings. "I am the Maestro," the man said. "Welcome to my humble abode." He gestured to the villa. "I know you will be happy here, my pretty purple friend. You, too, tomtomme. With the help of my own immense musical talent, your own more humble skills shall finally reach the audience they deserve."

The sound of a door scraping open interrupted him. Lorelei gasped: A small, sad-eyed girl had just emerged from a building across the courtyard.

"Serena!" she yelled, her voice free at last.

"Lorelei!" Serena cried, rushing forward. Four moplike creatures bounded along behind her, their tiny bright eyes peering out from beneath their shaggy fur. The largest of the creatures was yellow, the smallest blue, the other two orange and green. The citrustacks—how could Lorelei have forgotten them? The friendly, industrious little creatures were the only thing she and Serena had left from their former lives.

The Maestro raised his baton. "No!" Lorelei screamed.

But it was too late. A beam of blue light burst from the baton's tip. The light enveloped Serena, and she began to shrink before Lorelei's eyes. With a flick of his wrist, the Maestro magically lifted the now tiny Serena into the air and tossed her into the open music box.

Bongo banged his tail on the ground with alarm. The Maestro glanced at him.

"You want to go next, hmm?" He aimed the baton again. The tomtomme yipped as the blue light caught him and whisked him into the box as well.

Thwang!

Harmony reacted to Bongo's disappearance with a discordant batch of notes. The Maestro cried out, clamping both hands over his ears.

"Ow, what a hideous note!" he shouted, doubling over in pain.

Lorelei scooped up the citrustacks, which were whirling around in confusion near the music box. Then she ran toward the archway. "We have to get away!" she yelled to the horses.

Moonsprite took a few steps forward, and then stopped. She sent an urgent image of Bongo into Lorelei's mind.

Lorelei's eyes filled with tears. How could she make them understand? If they stayed here, they would be trapped just like poor Bongo . . . and Serena.

Dart's ears flattened back against his head as he glared at the Maestro. He snorted and pawed the ground. Then, lowering his head, he charged.

The Maestro recovered enough to raise his baton as the colt attacked. He wasn't

quick enough to aim the tip at Dart, but he was able to escape the colt's attack, using the baton against Dart's horn like a sword.

"Dart, be careful!" Lorelei shouted.

Dart spun on his haunches and came at the man again. The Maestro was better prepared this time, but the colt was quick and sure-footed. The blast of blue light missed its mark as Dart dodged to one side and then turned to make another thrust.

This time, instead of facing the colt with his baton, the Maestro took a step back and grabbed the music box. "No!" Lorelei cried, realizing what he was doing.

The Maestro met her gaze. "Don't worry, my dear," he said. "We'll meet again soon. I promise."

Then he slammed the music box lid shut. A blast of music filled the air, and there was a flash of light and a puff of smoke. When it cleared, the Maestro and the music box had vanished.

4

With the Maestro gone, his spell was broken. The villa was once again the dreary ruin it had been when they had first arrived. Lorelei sank down on the edge of the broken fountain, tears streaming down her face.

She looked up when she heard a snort of fear. Moonsprite was staring wide-eyed toward the horizon. The sun was setting, even though it had barely risen when they'd first reached the villa.

"That's the magic of the music box,"

Lorelei said wearily. "It makes time do strange things. There's no telling how long we've really been here."

Harmony turned to face her, ears flattened against her head. Lorelei braced herself for accusations to flood her mind, but there was nothing. Somehow, that was even worse.

"I'm so sorry," she said, her voice wavering. "It's like the Maestro said—I was under a spell. I didn't remember anything about him or why he'd sent me out. If I had, I never would have brought you here. Or poor Bongo, either." She wiped her eyes with the back of her hand.

Moonsprite sent a tentative question into her mind. Lorelei shook her head sadly.

"He's gone. The Maestro added him to his collection inside the music box. He'll be trapped there, let out only for performances, along with Serena."

The citrustacks wriggled in her arms. She'd almost forgotten grabbing them.

Feeling their familiar furry warmth made her smile sadly.

"At least you guys are free," she told them, opening her arms so they could bounce to the ground.

The citrustacks *boing*ed around the clearing, making joyful little *whoop! whoop!* noises. The foals eyed the little creatures warily.

"Surely you've seen citrustacks before?" Lorelei said. "They're the tidiest creatures in North of North. They can clean anything." She grimaced. "That's why the Maestro saved them from the fire that destroyed my family's home. You should have seen the inside of the music box when we first arrived! Serena and I had never seen such a mess."

Her heart dropped at the very mention of her sister's name. She couldn't stand the thought of Serena still being under the Maestro's power. But how could Lorelei ever free her without being recaptured herself? She glanced over and saw that the foals seemed to be debating among themselves. She thought she may have caught a glimpse of a thought from Harmony, having to do with saving Bongo. Suddenly, she felt a tiny ray of hope.

"I know where he's probably taking them," she offered. "The Festival of Lights. The Maestro has been talking about it for ages. It's supposed to be his biggest musical triumph yet."

Dart nickered. An image came to Lorelei: the three foals and their families walking toward the great festival. The little herd had been on its way there when Lorelei had encountered them.

Lorelei wasn't surprised. Every year, humans and horses and other creatures from all over North of North traveled to the town of Canter Hollow for the Festival of Lights, the joyful holiday that celebrated the form-ing of the Valkyrie Sisterhood so long ago.

"Oh, so we can look for Bongo and Serena there!" she said. "That is, if you'll let me go with you. . . ."

Moonsprite and Dart tilted their ears agreeably. But Harmony's still lay flat against her head in anger. Lorelei's heart sank. Harmony still suspected she'd led them to the Maestro on purpose. Would she ever trust Lorelei again?

She tentatively hummed a few bars of the song they'd shared earlier, hoping that might soften the filly's anger. But Harmony turned and walked away, heading for the trail back through the forest.

Lorelei sighed. She needed more than music to fix this. She fell into step as the others drifted after Harmony. The citrus-stacks bounced along as well.

The little group made its way back through the darkening forest. They were about halfway back to the meadow when the sound of flapping wings filled the air. A chill ran down Lorelei's spine.

"The crow!" she cried. "Oh no, not again!"

The foals snorted in alarm. But before any of them could react, something crashed through the trees and landed at their feet with a *plop!*

Lorelei nearly laughed with relief. It wasn't the crow after all. It was only a whiffle bear!

"Well, hello," she greeted the fuzzy, winged creature. Whiffle bears, although sometimes mischievous, were very friendly. This particular whiffle bear looked young. His fur was fuzzy and pale, and his large, butterflylike wings were just beginning to develop their full pink color.

The little bear sat up and brushed himself off. The green citrustack bounced over to help, quickly brushing every speck of dirt from the whiffle bear with his moplike body.

Finally, the whiffle bear stood up. Then he started capering around, half running and half flying, his eyes wide with excitement.

"I think he's trying to tell us something," Lorelei said. She watched carefully as the whiffle bear landed on a tree branch.

He pointed toward the foals and then off to his right. "It looks like he's seen your parents?"

The bear nodded vigorously. Then he held a paw above his eyes and pretended to scan the area.

"Your parents looked for you," Lorelei translated. "Where are they now?" she asked the whiffle bear.

He pointed in the opposite direction. West. Then he moved his paw in a large arc.

Lorelei slowly turned back to the horses. "I think he's saying they searched for you and then headed far to the west. They must have gone on to the festival." The whiffle bear flapped his wings eagerly and nodded. "That's strange," said Lorelei. "Do you know anything else? Why they didn't keep looking for their foals?" She glanced at the whiffle bear. He shook his head, and shrugged. Then he leaped up and took to the air, almost crashing into a branch or two before rising up through the treetops. Just like that, he was gone.

The foals looked at one another in horror. Lorelei shuddered. She didn't want to say it out loud. Could her friends' parents have really given up so easily? Could they truly have just *left* them?

5

*M*oonsprite and Dart hung their heads low as they walked. Harmony trailed behind the group. Lorelei could sense how abandoned the foals felt. And it was all her fault. If she hadn't brought them into the Maestro's trap . . .

"Okay, I know this is asking a lot since I got you into this mess. But we need to stick together now more than ever. We will travel west to Canter Hollow and look for your parents at the festival. And maybe once we find them, they can help us figure out how to find the Maestro and get my sister and Bongo back."

Moonsprite let out an uncertain snort. Dart glanced over, looking dubious. One of the citrustacks let out a soft *whoop!*

Only Harmony didn't respond. She kept striding forward, head stiff and ears slightly back. Lorelei bit her lip. Why couldn't the violet foal understand that she hadn't meant to hurt her or her friends?

She was still fretting over that when she became aware of the roar of a river just ahead. Soon they'd reached its banks. There was a steep drop-off, and the water churned violently.

"We'd better look for a safer place to cross," Lorelei said.

Harmony responded by turning and heading downstream. Lorelei opened her mouth to say that she thought the terrain seemed more promising upstream. But she held her tongue. Harmony didn't trust her as it was; the last thing Lorelei wanted was to make her even angrier by disagreeing.

And so they all walked downstream. Dart took the lead when the bushes grew thicker, pushing his way through the worst of them with his horn to clear the path. But the farther they went, the wilder the river got, full of rapids and whirlpools. Lorelei wondered uneasily if this might be one of the livelier tributaries of the Fastalon River that tumbled more and more recklessly downhill through the forest to burst into Horseshoe Bay. If so, traveling farther downriver was unlikely to be any safer to cross.

When they finally reached a relatively narrow spot, Dart stopped and whinnied impatiently. Lorelei knew how he felt. They'd wasted half the day looking for a spot to cross. Every minute they spent here was another minute that Serena and Bongo had to spend trapped by the Maestro.

"It still looks pretty rough," she said, surveying the raging river. Then she noticed a thick vine hanging from a nearby tree. "Hey, isn't that a cord vine? People use those as rope all the time. The vines are flexible but very strong." She tilted her head up, peering into the canopy to gauge how long the vine was. "If we can loop it onto a tree on the other side, we can hold onto it as we cross."

Even Harmony seemed to agree with the plan. The foals grabbed the vine in their teeth, helping Lorelei pull it down. Then the citrustacks scurried over its entire length, clearing away all the leaves and tendrils. Finally, Lorelei tied a large loop onto one end.

"Okay, let's see if I can lasso that branch over there." She twirled the loop over her head and then swung it out over the river, aiming for a jutting branch on the far side.

But tossing the heavy vine across the river turned out to be much harder than it looked. The first time, it barely cleared the near bank. The second attempt went only a little farther. Dart gave her a nudge with his muzzle. "What is it?" she panted, glancing at him, "I'm trying my best!"

Dart snaked his neck forward and grabbed the loop end of the vine in his teeth. Then he galloped straight toward the bank.

Moonsprite let out a whinny of alarm. Harmony's lyre clanged discordantly. Lorelei gasped as she realized what the colt meant to do. She instantly remembered Dart trying to fly on top of the hillock when they had first met.

"Dart, no!" she cried. "You can't fly over—it's too far!"

But the colt didn't hesitate. When he reached the edge, he leaped into the air. His wings beat wildly as he sailed over the water.

Lorelei held her breath. He was doing it!

Then she saw him lurch down toward the churning water. Harmony let out a

whinny of dismay, and the citrustacks bur-
bled worriedly, bouncing up and down.

Dart let out a determined snort. He
spread his wings as wide as they would go—
and they caught an air current, finally lifting
him up. He wobbled a bit once or twice, but
was able to glide the rest of the way to the
far bank.

"Way to go, Dart!" Lorelei shouted.
Moonsprite and Harmony whinnied and
bucked with excitement.

Lorelei tied her end of the vine to a
tree trunk. Dart wrapped his end around a
large tree on the other bank. Keeping the
rope clenched in his mouth, he backed away
from the tree, tightening the rope.

Harmony waded into the river first.
Using her teeth to keep hold of the vine,
she swam into the torrent. She let the vine
slide through her mouth, clamping down
occasionally to keep from being swept away.
Moonsprite was right behind her, doing the
same.

Lorelei picked up the citrustacks. "Will you be able to ride on my shoulders?" she asked. In reply, the blue citrustack nuzzled into the shaggy fur of the green one. When it had disappeared inside, the green one disappeared inside the orange one. Then the orange citrustack climbed into the yellow one's fur. Lorelei smiled. She'd nearly forgotten why the creatures were called citrustacks!

"Okay, hold on tight," she said, tucking the stack into her blouse. Then she followed the foals into the water.

The water was shockingly cold, but Lorelei kicked out strongly, hanging on to the vine with both hands. Soon they were all more than halfway across the river.

"Almost there!" she called out encouragingly.

Crack!

Suddenly, the rope went slack. Through the spray, Lorelei saw Dart tumble backward and realized what had

happened—the tree he'd looped it around had broken! Lorelei hardly had time to scream before water filled her mouth, and she felt herself being swept away by the raging current.

*L*orelei struggled to keep her head above water as the river carried her downstream. A few yards behind her, the two fillies were struggling against the current. She could feel the citrustacks trembling against her chest.

There was a loud whinny from the shoreline. Blinking the water out of her eyes, she saw Dart galloping along, keeping pace with them. But there was nothing he could do.

Just ahead was a sharp turn in the river. Lorelei angled herself as best she could. She hoped the current wouldn't slam her against the bank or any of the tall, jagged rocks jutting up out of the water.

Then she realized that perhaps those rocks could be their salvation. She kicked harder, swimming into the turn. As she neared the bend, she reached out for one of the rocks. Her hand slid off its slimy surface. She tried again and caught the next one. It was rough and jagged, its sharp edges digging into her palm. But she ignored the pain, twisting around and extending her other arm.

"Harmony!" she shouted. "This way!"

The wide-eyed foal swam toward the girl, aiming for her outstretched hand. When she was within reach, Lorelei grabbed onto Harmony's mane. The filly's weight almost yanked her grip loose, but she dug in even harder. Harmony kept swimming against the current, taking some of the pressure off. But when Moonsprite swept past and grabbed onto Harmony's tail with her teeth, Lorelei once again felt her hand slip.

"Swim harder!" she cried, hanging on with everything she had. She knew she was the only thing keeping all three of them—plus the citrustacks—from being swept downriver.

Harmony let out a determined whinny. Then she began swimming harder than ever, pulling Moonsprite with her. A second later, Lorelei felt a chunk of dirt or rock swish past her ankle. Harmony's foreleg had just struck ground!

That was all it took. The filly lunged for the shallows, pulling the other two with her. Soon all three of them were climbing the rocky bank on shaky legs.

Dart was there to meet them. He whinnied anxiously, running around in circles with his wings flapping wildly.

Lorelei collapsed onto the grass, never so happy to feel solid ground beneath her. She tugged on her blouse, and the citrustacks popped out and unstacked themselves. They looked rather bedraggled—like colorful little wet mops—but not for long. Each of them squirted a stream of water out of its unseen mouth. Then, like four fuzzy little dogs, they all shook at once. Just like that, they were back to their usual woolly selves.

Whoop! Whoop! They bounced around Lorelei so energetically that she couldn't help but chuckle.

"Is everyone all right?" she asked wearily, pushing herself to a sitting position.

Moonsprite walked over and lowered her head, nuzzling Lorelei's cheek with her soft, damp muzzle. Grateful feelings filled Lorelei's mind.

"You're welcome." She reached up to scratch the white filly's poll. "But it's okay. I owed you one. If it wasn't for me, none of you would've been in this mess to start with."

She shot a slightly nervous glance at Harmony. To her surprise, Harmony was gazing back with uncertain eyes. When she caught Lorelei's glance, she immediately turned away. But this time her ears were floppy and her body relaxed.

Lorelei's heart jumped. Maybe things

weren't hopeless between her and the violet filly after all. . . .

"Okay," she said, standing up and doing her best to wring out her clothes. "I suppose we'd better keep moving."

By late afternoon, dark thunderclouds had rolled in. The little group found shelter in a snug hollow among the huge, gnarled roots of an elm so ancient that Lorelei imagined it must have been a sapling during the days of the great Valkyrie leader Sigga Rolanddotter. By the time sheets of rain started drenching the forest, they were cozy and warm.

Still, Lorelei couldn't help noting that Harmony held herself a little apart from the group, even in their close quarters. Trying to comfort herself by resting her head against Moonsprite's flank as the citrustacks cuddled around her, Lorelei drifted off to sleep.

Sometime later, a boom of thunder awakened her. She gasped and sat upright, trembling from the dream she'd just had. In it, the Maestro had trapped Serena inside a crystal flute and then tossed it into the river. He laughed as he watched Lorelei race helplessly along the bank trying to keep her sister in sight.

Lorelei rubbed her eyes, wishing bleakly that she and her sister had been born without musical talent. Perhaps then the Maestro never would have taken an interest in them and they would still be living happily at home. . . . Suddenly sensing that someone else was awake, she glanced around. The next flash of lightning revealed that Harmony was sitting up watching her.

"Sorry," Lorelei whispered over the sound of Dart's soft snores and the gentle burbling of the snoozing citrustacks. "I hope I didn't wake you. I had a nightmare." She shuddered as the dream flashed back through her mind.

Harmony tilted her head to one side as if listening. Then she sent a picture into Lorelei's mind, shy and hesitant. In it, Lorelei saw herself nestled beside the violet filly.

"Really?" she whispered, fearing she'd misunderstood.

Harmony snorted softly. Carefully disentangling herself from the citrustacks, Lorelei crept across the hollow. Harmony let out a sigh, sending soothing feelings toward her. Lorelei rested her head on the filly's side, breathing in the warm scent of her silky coat. The lyre began to play, soft as a butterfly's wings, harmonizing with the rain. Seconds later, Lorelei drifted away into a dreamless sleep.

7

The group awakened to a bright new day. The storm had passed, and sunlight glistened off the lingering droplets, turning every leaf and stone into a sparkling kaleidoscope. After a quick breakfast—rain-plump grass for the foals, a handful of berries for Lorelei, dirt and cobwebs for the citrus-stacks—they continued on their journey.

By the time the warm morning sun had burned off most of the moisture, the forest was beginning to thin. Finally, the narrow track they were following ended at the edge of a broad, well-worn dirt road.

"Civilization!" Lorelei exclaimed. "And look, this road goes west. We'll be in Canter Hollow in no time now."

Dart reared, kicking out his front legs in excitement and almost bumping into Moonsprite in the process. She sent out a cranky image showing Dart having fallen over backward and flailing on his back like a turtle.

Lorelei laughed, feeling more optimistic than she had in ages. On a bright, clean morning like this, with friends at her side, anything seemed possible—even finding the foals' parents and rescuing Serena and Bongo.

"Come on," she said. "Let's go!"

Lorelei's stomach rumbled as she walked. Those berries hadn't filled her up at all, especially since she hadn't eaten a thing for most of the previous day. She hummed a song to distract herself from her hunger, and after a moment Harmony joined in, her golden lyre strumming a descant.

But even that couldn't keep Lorelei's

mind off her empty belly for long. After a few minutes she even imagined she *smelled* food.

Then they rounded a bend and she realized she wasn't imagining things. An abandoned farm stood at the side of the road. In front of the barn, a campfire sizzled and crackled, with a pot of bubbling oatmeal cooking over it.

A man with blond hair, a goatee, and a long pointed nose sat beside the fire strumming a mandolin. He wore tall boots, leather pants, and a ruffled canary-colored tunic.

"Greetings!" he called, setting down his mandolin and hopping to his feet. "What a fine morning, is it not?"

"Indeed. And a good morning to you," Lorelei answered.

She drifted toward the fire, drawn by the enticing scent of the oatmeal. The foals followed.

"My name is Burke Cawfield," the man said. He nodded his head, causing the

golden feather in his cap to bob.

"I'm Lorelei. These are my friends, Moonsprite, Dart, and Harmony." Noticing a flash of color nearby, she smiled. "Oh, and the citrustacks, of course."

The citrustacks had been riding along on Dart's back. But when Burke stepped forward to look at them, they tumbled away to hide behind Moonsprite, whooping in alarm.

Burke chuckled. "Shy little things, aren't they?"

Lorelei blinked in surprise. "I don't know what's wrong with them," she said, a little embarrassed by the citrustacks' behavior. "They're usually very friendly."

"Never mind," Burke said. "Perhaps they're hungry. I have plenty of delicious oatmeal, made with my special honey oats." He gestured to the steaming pot. "Would you like some?"

Lorelei's mouth watered at the scent of the oatmeal. "Well, if you're sure you have enough . . ."

Burke pulled four bowls and a large grain bag out of his pack. He dipped one of the bowls into the pot, scooping out a healthy portion of oatmeal, which he handed to Lorelei along with a spoon.

"Perhaps just some fresh oats for you three?" he asked the foals with a slight bow.

The young horses' ears perked in eager agreement. Burke dipped the remaining three bowls into the sack of grain.

The oatmeal was delicious. Lorelei was certain she'd never tasted anything so good, at least not in a long, long time. The Maestro rarely fed them anything but stale bread crusts and cold leftovers from his own meals.

I can't wait to find Serena, Lorelei thought, as she licked her lips. *The first thing we'll do is eat a big, delicious meal like this. And afterward we'll sing because we want to, not because the Maestro is forcing us with his magic!*

Noticing that the citrustacks were still hanging back, whooping softly to one another, she scooped up a spoonful of oatmeal and held it out. "Would you like some oatmeal, little ones?"

The green one eyed the food, and then hid behind the others. The blue one bobbed up and down uncertainly. *Whoop!* he muttered. Then all four of them moved a little farther away.

Lorelei shrugged and glanced at Burke. "They don't really eat people food," she explained. "They prefer dirt and dust and stuff like that. And they especially love sweets. I guess oatmeal is too healthy for them!"

"Never mind," Burke said cheerfully. He was sitting, watching them eat with his hands folded in his lap.

"Aren't you going to have some of your oatmeal?" Lorelei asked, taking another bite herself.

"I've already had my fill." He picked up his mandolin. "Here, let me play you something to eat by. They say music aids in digestion." He began to pluck a slow, beautiful tune.

Lorelei scraped up the last bite of her oatmeal. She set the bowl down, feeling content, relaxed, and even a little sleepy. Leaning back against a log, she stifled a burp.

Nearby, the foals had finished their oats. All three of them looked as groggy as Lorelei felt. They swayed on their long legs, and Dart had to flap his little wings to keep from tipping right over.

Whoop! Whoop! The citrustacks bounced closer, sounding worried. Lorelei felt their fuzzy warmth on her foot, but she was too tired to reach down and pat them.

"I'm so sleepy," she mumbled, fighting to keep her eyes open. "Why am I so sleepy all of a sudden?"

She cast a blurry gaze toward Burke and saw that he was grinning from ear to ear.

"Don't let me keep you up, friends," he chortled. "And don't you little mischief makers try to wake them, either."

With that, he lunged forward and grabbed at the citrustacks. The fuzzy creatures squealed with fright. Lorelei knew she should do something, but her entire body felt as heavy as Mount Whitemantle. Her eyes opened slightly as she heard a jangling chord, and she saw that Harmony had just collapsed to the ground.

Her mind felt as if it had been filled with molasses. Keeping her eyes open was just too much effort. She let them drift shut again. Then there was only darkness.

8

*L*orelei slowly opened her eyes. For a second all remained dark. Then her vision began to adjust, and she saw that she was now indoors. Dusty cobwebs dangled from stout wooden rafters. Stale straw lined the floor. The only light came from the moon peeping in through cracks in the boards and a glowworm or two clinging to the ceiling.

She groaned as she pushed herself upright. Her head was throbbing so much that she nearly had to lie down again.

A snort came out of the dimness

nearby. Squinting over, she saw all three foals struggling to sit up as well.

"That man, Burke," she said, her voice hoarse. "He put something in our food! Is everyone all right?"

Dart snorted, and Moonsprite gave a shaky nicker. Harmony didn't answer, and when Lorelei glanced at her, she saw the violet foal's head hanging even lower than the others.

"Harmony, what's wrong?" Lorelei wobbled to her feet and took a step closer. Then she gasped, realizing the answer to her own question. The filly's floating lyre was gone!

Harmony raised her head and gazed at Lorelei with sad eyes. Lorelei's own eyes filled with tears as she felt the grief and agony emanating from the violet filly. For Harmony, losing the lyre was like losing a part of herself. If Lorelei's voice had been torn from her throat, it would have hurt as much. Why would that man, Burke, do such a thing? How could anyone be so cruel?

"Try not to worry," she said softly, stepping forward and touching Harmony gently on her velvety nose. "We'll get it back."

The other two foals had climbed to their feet by now. Dart snorted his agreement, stamping his foot angrily. Moonsprite sidled closer to Harmony, nuzzling at her gently.

Lorelei glanced around. "We must be in that old barn we saw near the campfire," she mused aloud. Walking over to the door, she gave it a push. It didn't budge. "Feels like it's barred from the outside," she told the horses.

She looked around for another exit. But the only other opening in the old but sturdy barn was a grimy window located high up on the wall. It was not only well out of reach, but also too narrow even for the slender Lorelei to squeeze through, let alone the horses. Still, she touched the wall, wondering if she could find a way to climb up there and look out. Her fingers landed right in a dusty cobweb.

"Ugh," she said, quickly wiping her hand on her leggings. "Too bad the citru-stacks aren't here. This place could use a good cleaning." She winced at the foggy memory of Burke lunging for the fuzzy little creatures. What did he want with the citru-stacks? For that matter, what did he want with any of them—or Harmony's lyre?

Just then, something wriggled in her pocket. She jumped and let out a scream, envisioning the enormous, dusty spider that surely belonged with all these cobwebs. Then she heard a muffled but familiar whoop.

"Oh!" she cried, as the smallest citru-stack, the blue one, popped out and *boing*ed to the floor. "How did you get in there?"

The blue citrustack bounced up and down, greeting them all with friendly whoops. Despite the seriousness of the sit-uation, Lorelei smiled. She was glad that at least one of her little friends had escaped Burke's clutches!

Dart let out a whinny, and then trot-ted over to stand below the window. Lorelei held her breath as he sent out an image of the citrustack bouncing up to open it.

"Hey, can you do us a favor?" Lorelei asked the citrustack. She explained Dart's idea. With a quick *Whoop! Whoop!* the citrustack *boing*ed up onto Dart's back and then up the wall. He landed easily on the windowsill. Moments later, he was rubbing busily against the glass.

"Don't clean it!" Lorelei called up to him with a wry smile. "Open it! See if there's a way to get us out of here. Please?"

Whoop! The half cleaned window creaked open. The citrustack disappeared through it.

Lorelei held her breath, waiting. For a moment there was silence. Then came a soft shuffling sound outside. Lorelei guessed that the citrustack was trying to figure out how to open the heavy barn door.

Before long, he reappeared on the windowsill. *Whoop!* he chirped sadly.

"Too heavy?" Lorelei guessed, her heart sinking.

Then she felt a new image in her mind—a picture of Burke. It was from Moonsprite.

"I think she wants to know if Burke is out there," Lorelei guessed. At the filly's nod, everyone looked at the citrustack. "Did you see him?" Lorelei asked.

This time the citrustack's whoops were happier. It seemed that Burke was nowhere in sight. Lorelei was glad to hear it, although she wasn't sure what difference it made. Then she noticed that Harmony and Dart were both staring at Moonsprite. The white foal looked nervous. She stepped forward into the beam of moonlight the citrustack's cleaning had allowed in through the window.

Lorelei gasped as she saw Moonsprite's pale coat glisten in the moonlight—and then fade. Within seconds, Lorelei could see right through her!

"Wow!" she murmured.

Whoop! the citrustack agreed, bouncing down onto Lorelei's shoulder.

Dart gave an encouraging nicker. Moonsprite's nostrils flared as she took in a deep breath. Then she walked toward the wall—and passed right through it! Lorelei had never seen anything so amazing. True, she'd heard there were certain magical horses—specters, they were called—who could become incorporeal at will. But she hadn't realized until now that Moonsprite was among their number. The white filly's talents included more than just dancing!

Soon they all heard the sound of the bar across the door scraping back. Once it was out of the way, Lorelei and the other two foals helped push it open. They were free!

The moon was high, and the surrounding forest was alive with the sound of crickets. Lorelei glanced around and saw a light through the trees.

"Look," she whispered. "That must be Burke. Let's go see if he has the other citrustacks."

They made their way through

underbrush, following the light. As they got closer, Lorelei saw that it was coming through the window of a farmhouse. She noticed that the walls of the house were caving in on one side, and a tree seemed to be sprouting through part of the roof!

Lorelei tiptoed up to the house, perched herself on a tree stump, and carefully peeked inside. Burke was sitting at a cobweb-ridden table staring at a glass case with a handle on top. The other three citrustacks were trapped inside, *boing*ing helplessly against the glass.

A bird was perched on the handle, black as pitch with a long, sharp beak. As Lorelei watched, Burke leaned closer to it.

"Listen, my friend," he told the bird. "Fly quickly and tell the Maestro that I have the girl, the citrustacks, *and* the little purple horse's harp." He gestured to something else on the table. Lorelei's eyes widened as she saw Harmony's lyre. Its luminous purple glow had faded so much that she hadn't noticed it at first.

Burke leaned back in his chair with his arms behind his head and smiled. "And tell the Maestro that it was just so easy! All I had to do was tell their parents that I'd seen their little horsies heading in the direction of the Festival of Lights. I couldn't have any adult horses getting in the way, of course. And now I've got them all just where I want them."

She jumped down from the window, her mind reeling. So Burke worked for the Maestro! And worse, he had tricked the foals' parents into leaving them behind! She hurried back and told the others what she'd learned. "Your parents didn't just give up on looking for you. They were tricked by Burke! And he works for the Maestro! Burke must have some magic of his own to have tracked us," she whispered. "But never mind. We have magic, too, and I have a plan. . . ."

She quickly outlined what she had in mind. Dart snorted his agreement right away. Moonsprite looked nervous, but nodded. Then Lorelei looked to Harmony. They'd seemed to bond the night before. But had she truly won the violet filly's trust?

Harmony closed her eyes for a moment. Then she opened them again and reached out to nuzzle Lorelei with her velvety muzzle. A feeling of agreement and trust washed through the girl's mind, and Lorelei smiled gratefully.

"Good," she whispered. "Then let's do it!"

Soon they were all in position—Harmony and Lorelei by the window, Dart near the front door, and Moonsprite in between. Then Lorelei whistled softly, a brief tune that might easily be mistaken for some night bird's call.

At that signal, Moonsprite stepped out of the shadows into the moonlight. As before, she faded and became translucent. Lorelei and Harmony watched as she moved through the wall and into the room with Burke.

The man didn't notice her at first. But when he did, he sprang out of his chair as if he'd been stung by a hundred bees. *"Yiiiiii-ahhhhhh!* A ghost! A horse spirit!" he shouted.

Moonsprite bucked and ran around the room. She passed through fallen boxes and broken chairs. As she came around again, she passed right though Burke himself.

"Yaaaaaaaaaah!" he screamed with fright.

"Now, Harmony," Lorelei whispered.

The filly closed her eyes, and spooky music filled the air. The lyre was playing. Harmony strained and Lorelei began humming quietly, hoping her own music might help the filly control the lyre from this greater distance. Sure enough, the lyre's music grew louder. Its strings magically plucked eerie-sounding chords as it rose off the table. Burke had to duck as it floated past his head toward the window.

"This place is bewitched!" he shouted.

Just then, Dart rammed through the crumbling front door. He galloped across

the room, aiming his stubby horn. Burke let out another howl as the horn connected with his backside.

At that, Lorelei couldn't contain herself. She burst into laughter.

Burke's head whipped around. "You!" he hissed, spying her through the window. "I should have guessed—the old man said you're a troublemaker. Well, you're not the only one with a few tricks up your sleeve!"

He raised his arms. The baggy sleeves of his yellow shirt billowed in the candle's light. Burke crouched down and then leaped up into the air.

"Remember me?" he cried—or, rather, cawed. For he had suddenly transformed into the enormous yellow crow!

*L*orelei scrambled away from the window. She ran as fast as she could, expecting to feel those cruel talons biting into her flesh at any moment. . . .

But Burke didn't seem interested in catching her. He burst through the window with the citrustacks' cage clutched in his talons. Together with the smaller black bird, he flapped up and disappeared into the night.

Lorelei's shoulders slumped as she realized that the citrustacks, like her sister and Bongo, would soon be back under the control of the Maestro. "Well, now we know how Burke found us," she mumbled as the others gathered around her. "He must have tracked us in his crow form and then set his trap."

Her eyes filled with tears. With such devious helpers on his side, how could she ever hope to defeat the Maestro?

Then she noticed that the others were all watching her, waiting for her to figure out what to do next. She couldn't let them down.

Not like I let down Serena, she thought. *Or poor little Bongo. Or the other three citrustacks . . .*

She did her best to banish such thoughts. At least they'd retrieved Harmony's lyre. That was something, wasn't it? If they could do that, they could figure out a way to rescue the others, too!

"Come on," she said, turning back toward the road. "We may as well keep walking. I suspect we're all going to end up at the same place—the festival. We'll figure out what to do on the way."

* * *

By midmorning they'd made good progress despite a steady drizzle that started soon after sunrise. Lorelei wasn't sure how much farther they had to travel, but she began to hope they might reach Canter Hollow by evening.

Then she heard an unwelcome rumble in the distance. "Oh, no," she said, glancing up at the sky. "Is that thunder?"

The wet ground vibrated beneath her feet as the rumble grew louder. The others felt it, too. Dart let out a snort, and the citrustack bounced onto Lorelei's shoulder, whooping nervously.

"Can it be an earthquake?" Lorelei cried.

She jumped back as the rain-drenched trees on one side of the road shook, even though there was no wind. What was going on?

The trees parted, bending in opposite directions as if giant invisible hands were pushing them apart. Lorelei's eyes widened as she saw something rapidly approaching down the newly created path.

"Out of the way!" she shouted, leaping behind a nearby boulder. The foals scurried after her.

They were just in time. An enormous herd of green ponies leaped into view. They galloped across the road and into the forest on the other side, where the trees and bushes were parting before them. The ponies kept coming, more than Lorelei could have imagined, a steady stream of them seeming to pour from one side to the other.

But finally the stream ended. The trees snapped back to their original positions . . . most of them, anyway. Lorelei noticed a few still bent down. For a second she thought the ponies had broken them. Then she saw that standing there, nearly lost in the green of the forest, were five of the green ponies. They were watching Lorelei and her friends curiously.

The rest of the ponies had moved so fast that Lorelei had barely been able to make out what they were. Now she was able to get a better look at these ponies' dark green coats, which glistened as if they'd been sprayed with a fine mist. Their deep blue eyes were the color of the sea, and their manes and tails were woven with flowing vines and leaves. Now Lorelei recognized them from tales her parents had told when she was very young.

"You—you're dew ponies!" she blurted out.

The old stories flooded her mind. Dew ponies normally traveled in the early morning hours when dew covered the leaves and grass. The ponies' magic gave them the ability to part the wet vegetation, allowing them to gallop through even the densest forest like a hot knife through butter.

"Of course," she murmured. "They're using the rain to travel toward the festival."

Four of the lingering dew ponies had jumped back at the first sound of her voice. Lorelei wasn't surprised. Dew ponies were said to be among the shyest equines in

North of North.

But the fifth pony held her ground. She even took a step closer, staring curiously at the travelers.

"Hello," Lorelei greeted her. "I'm Lorelei. These are my friends." She introduced the others.

The dew pony tossed her head. Suddenly, Lorelei's mind was filled with the image of a wet leaf. A drop of water dripped from its tip.

"It's a drop of dew," she guessed breathlessly. "Is that your name? Dew-drop?"

The pony nickered, sounding delighted. Lorelei smiled.

"It's wonderful to meet you, Dew-drop," she said. "Please, could you tell us—are we almost to Canter Hollow?"

Dewdrop shook her head, spray from her thick mane mixing with the rain. She sent the image of a map into Lorelei's mind.

Lorelei's heart sank. If she understood the pony correctly, they still had miles and miles to go. They would not only be unable to reach the festival today, but be lucky to get there by tomorrow!

Harmony nickered urgently to the dew pony. Lorelei wasn't sure what she was saying, but Dewdrop seemed to understand. A moment later both horses sent a vision: Lorelei riding Dewdrop as she galloped through the dense forest, with Harmony and the other foals running along in their wake.

"Really?" Lorelei cried, overwhelmed as she understood the pony's generous offer. "Oh, thank you! That would be wonderful! Thank you so much!"

Soon the amazing vision was a reality. Lorelei's legs clung tightly against Dewdrop's rain-slick side, her hands buried in the pony's thick mane, as the five dew ponies took off. It was scary at first to see Dewdrop careen directly toward a cluster of trees. Several times, Lorelei squeezed her eyes shut tight in terror. But she eventually got used to it, accepting that the trees would part to let them through.

After a few minutes, their little group caught up with the larger herd. Riding Dewdrop among hundreds of her fellow ponies felt a little like diving headlong over Teardrop Falls, or so Lorelei imagined. Spray coated her, and the waves of ponies ebbed and flowed on every side. Glancing back, she could catch only occasional glimpses of Harmony, Dart, and Moonsprite galloping along. The blue citrustack spent the whole ride tucked into her shirt, whooping softly and holding on tight. Lorelei wasn't sure how fast they were going, but she suspected that the ponies' speed and their shortcut directly through the forest would get them to Canter Hollow quickly. She just hoped the rain kept coming until they got there!

All too soon, the exhilarating ride ended. The ponies drifted to a stop, like a wave reaching up onto the beach and then losing energy. Lorelei slid down, her legs quivering with the exertion of holding on.

"Thank you so much, my friend," she

said, rubbing Dewdrop on her wet, glossy green neck. "I'll never, ever forget that ride."

When she finally took in the scene before her, she nearly lost her breath. There was Trails End and the town of Canter Hollow spread out before them like a sparkling jewel. The statues of Bella and Bello stood regally against the setting sun. Teardrop Lake glistened from under the boughs of the great World Tree. The towers of Rolandsgaard Castle sparkled. She couldn't wait to see it all close up. But first, Lorelei and her friends had some very important business to take care of at the festival.

The Festival of Lights was like nothing Lorelei had ever seen. Throngs of people and horses were everywhere she looked, seeming to stretch from the tiny hamlet of Canter Hollow all the way across the festival grounds to the base of Rolandsgaard Castle. People laughed and talked and sang. Children splashed happily in puddles left by the rain, which had finally tapered off. Horses nickered and pranced, greeting long lost friends and strangers alike with equal good cheer. Other magical creatures were everywhere, including some that Lorelei had never seen before except in books—a miniature three-tailed pufferfox, a droopy-eared gemdigger dog. Peddlers hawked their wares, their voices blending together like music. Strings of lights were just blinking on, adding a colorful touch to the darkening evening sky. The scents of food and flowers were everywhere, and somewhere in the distance a band was playing. Lorelei saw her favorite treat—strawberry-flavored bovo milk—being sold at a stand and smiled at the childhood memory.

"Now what?" Lorelei wondered, amazed. She had performed for some large crowds under the Maestro's control, but nothing like this! How were they ever going to find the foals' parents, let alone her sister and the other prisoners?

Dewdrop had already disappeared into the crowd with the rest of the dew ponies. Lorelei huddled with the three foals and the blue citrustack, feeling very small at the huge festival. She glanced up toward the giant horse heads carved in Mount Whitemantle in the distance, wishing the statues of the legend-ary horses Bella and Bello could tell her what to do. But no, she would have to figure it out herself.

As she looked around, Lorelei noticed a few passersby giving her strange looks. When the citrustack whooped and nudged her, she understood why. After their wild ride through the wet forest, she and the foals were filthy!

"Okay, little guy," she said with a chuckle. "Do your thing."

The citrustack whooped happily and then went to work. Before long he had Lore-lei and her friends sparkling clean. Then he bounced to the ground, shaking off the mois-ture he'd collected in a shower of sparkles. A few curious festivalgoers watched, laughing and clapping appreciatively.

"That's a citrustack for you," chortled a bearded man. "Always making the world a cleaner place. Now you're fit for the festival!"

Whoop! Whoop! the citrustack responded bashfully, bouncing into Lorelei's pocket.

Lorelei smiled at the man. "Excuse

me, but perhaps you could help us," she said. "We're looking for some horses—"

"Aye, you're in luck, then." The man chuckled. "Must be over a thousand horses here already."

Lorelei bit her lip and glanced at her friends. Then she had another idea. "We're also looking for a man," she said. "A musician. His name is the Maestro."

The man shrugged. "Take your pick. All the finest musicians in the land are here, too." Just then someone called to him, and he wandered off.

Lorelei sighed and glanced at her friends. "I suppose all we can do is start searching."

By the time the moon rose, she was feeling hopeless. They'd been wandering around for hours, with no glimpse of the foals' parents or the Maestro. She stopped and looked around. They were near the edge of the festival grounds. A raucous bunch of people and horses were nearby playing some sort of relay race.

Onlookers cheered loudly as food vendors and a strolling minstrel added to the cacophony.

Then a familiar sound pierced through the confusion. It was just a note or two, but the sweet voice jolted Lorelei to her very core. "That's Serena!" she cried.

At that moment the relay racers let out another cheer, swallowing up her sister's voice. Lorelei raced past them, straining her ears. Where had it come from?

The foals came, too, their ears rotating alertly. Harmony let out a snort and then took off at a trot.

Lorelei ran after her, her heart pounding. She hoped the filly's keener ears really had found her sister's voice in the clamor. Then she gasped as she caught it again—faint, but definitely familiar!

As they wound through the masses of festivalgoers, Serena's voice grew. After a while they could hear a rhythmic beat accompanying the song—Bongo!

"Come on!" Lorelei cried, taking the lead.

The crowd thinned as they neared the cliffs edging off the Fastalon River. Here on the fringes the festivalgoers were mostly resting, talking in small groups, and so on. But just upriver, Lorelei saw another crowd gathered around a shabby stage on which stood a familiar stooped figure.

"The Maestro!" Lorelei gasped. Fear flooded her at the sight of her former captor. "There they are!"

The Maestro had set up his traveling show right at the edge of the steep drop-off to the river far below. It was a lovely spot, but nobody was admiring the view. The audience was watching Serena as she stood on the stage beside the Maestro, her voice pouring sweetly over the festival grounds. Bongo thumped along beside her. Nearby, an elderly man with a violin and a golden-stringed, sad-eyed harp seal played along as well. Lorelei's eyes welled with tears at the sight of them. In all her worry about her sister, she'd nearly forgotten about the Mae-stro's other prisoners, the ones she'd lured to him on earlier trips out of the music box.

Speaking of the box . . .

Her gaze wandered around the stage until she spotted it. The wooden music box was standing open upon a stool near one side.

The song ended, and the audience clapped politely. The Maestro stepped forward, pulling out his magical monocle. Peering through it at the crowd, he began to sing:

I'm the greatest musician in the land.
If you agree, please lend a hand.
Coins, jewels, anything you can spare,
Place them in the basket . . . right over there.

Burke stepped into view, holding out a pole with a large basket attached. He extended it over the audience, and the people seemed all too eager to fill it.

Lorelei was surprised—she'd never seen this part of the show. "Usually we play inside a hall or in a small village," she murmured, more to herself than her friends. "The Maestro sends us back into the music box before this part. But I suppose here, he's afraid the rest of the festival may lure away his audience if he doesn't enchant them right away." She clenched her fists, angrier than ever now that she'd seen the swindle first-hand. "This has to stop—now!"

Harmony strummed an anxious chord, but Lorelei barely heard it. She raced forward, pushing through the crowd. When she reached the front, she hopped onto the stage. "This man is tricking you," she shouted at the audience. "Don't listen to him. Don't give him anything!"

"Lorelei!" Serena cried. "Look out!"

Lorelei glanced back and saw the Maestro grinning at her. "Welcome back, my dear," he hissed. His monocle swirled, aiming right at her.

Nooooo! Lorelei tried to resist, but it was futile. She felt the magic seeping into her mind. After that, all she could feel was an urge to sing.

She opened her mouth, beautiful notes pouring out. Serena, Bongo, and the others joined in with the sound as the enchanted crowd oohed and aahed.

Thwaaaang!

A horrible sound filled the air, drowning out the music. Audience members groaned or cried out; many covered their ears. Harmony pushed through the crowd, her lyre floating above her. It played the most awful chords Lorelei had ever heard.

Thwang! Thring! Thwoooong!

"Oh, how horrible!" the Maestro wailed. "Make it stop!"

Still, he had learned from his last encounter with the magical filly. Although he was doubled over in pain, he kept his monocle firmly in place.

Somewhere in Lorelei's mind, she understood what was happening. She struggled against the spell, but it was still too strong. Feeling helpless, she watched Harmony leap onto the stage. The filly whinnied and reared up. Her lyre played a

final horrible chord, louder than all the rest.

Twuuuuaaaaaaaangggggg!

The Maestro yelped as his monocle shattered. Lorelei's own thoughts and feelings rushed back, freed from the terrible magic. The audience was freed from the spell, too. They glanced around in confusion.

"Look at what you did, you horrible creature!" The Maestro threw the broken monocle to the ground and snatched up the music box and his baton. "You haven't seen the last of me!"

"Noooo!" Lorelei cried, as he turned the baton on Serena and the other musicians, whisking them back into the box. "Stop him!"

11

Lorelei and Harmony both lunged forward. But the Maestro was too far away. They'd never reach him in time!

Suddenly, Moonsprite materialized right behind the Maestro. Lorelei gasped. She hadn't even noticed the ghostly filly sneaking up to him!

"Go, Moonsprite!" she cheered, as the filly trumpeted in the Maestro's ear, startling him so much that he dropped the music box. It skidded across the stage upside down and fell off the edge.

"Horses!" the Maestro spat out.

"What good are they, anyway?"

He turned his baton toward Moon-sprite. But she disappeared again, leaving him cursing and spinning around, baton in hand.

The audience cheered uncertainly. Lorelei realized they must think this was all part of the act.

"No!" she cried, trying to make herself heard over the shouts. "He's a bad man! Please, you have to help us!"

"Sigga's sword!" a young man swore cheerfully. "This is the best show I've seen at this festival so far!"

Lorelei turned, ready to race across the stage to retrieve the music box. But the Maestro stepped into her path. "Looks like you brought back the rest of my new musicians after all," he said with a sneer. "Couldn't stay away, could you?"

"That's not why we're here!" Lorelei glared at him. "Let Serena and the others go!"

The Maestro chortled. "I think not!" he exclaimed, aiming his baton. "But don't worry, you and your sweet sister shall be reunited soon en—*Oof!*"

"Dart!" Lorelei cried.

The black colt had just charged the Maestro from behind, knocking him over. Now he stood over him, pawing a challenge.

"How dare you!" the Maestro exclaimed, leaping to his feet and facing off against Dart with the baton. "I let you off easy last time. But I think now I'd better teach you a lesson!"

Dart batted the baton aside with his horn. The Maestro swept it back into position. Dart lunged. The Maestro parried. The audience applauded as the pair dueled. Everyone still seemed to think this was part of the show. In fact, more and more people and horses were beginning to gather around the stage.

Lorelei glanced around. Moonsprite and Harmony were standing there, looking uncertain what to do next. Burke was climbing onto the stage, watching the Maestro and Dart. Out of the corner of her eye, Lorelei saw the blue citrustack bouncing toward the back of the stage. A moment later he disappeared over the edge.

She had no idea what he was doing—until she saw him reappear seconds later followed by his three colorful friends! Lorelei guessed that the citrustacks' glass prison had been hidden back there.

The four citrustacks bounced onto the stage, unnoticed by most of the others. Then they started *boing*ing up and down.

"Whoop! Whoop! Whoop!" they cried out, louder and louder.

The Maestro shot them an irritated glance. "Burke," he barked out. "Do something about those nasty little beasts!"

"Yes, Maestro." Burke strode toward the bouncing citrustacks, an evil glint in his eye.

Whoop! Whoop!

Lorelei blinked, glancing back over her shoulder. Where had that sound come from? She gasped as she saw several unfamiliar citrustacks bouncing up and down over the heads of the crowd. No, more than several—dozens! And then hundreds! Citrustacks were coming from every corner of the festival, summoned by the original four's call!

Burke swore as he saw citrustacks of every color of the rainbow coming at him from every direction. His eyes widened as they hopped on top of one another, forming a pyramid of citrustacks that towered over him.

The Maestro parried one of Dart's attacks, and then glanced over. "I thought I told you to do something about those things!" he yelled at Burke.

"Forget it!" Burke cried out. "You're on your own!" With that, he threw out his arms, transformed into the yellow crow, and flew away.

The Maestro cursed. Moving forward suddenly, he knocked Dart off balance just long enough to rush past him. By now, most of the citrustacks had bounced back offstage.

Only the original four were left—with the blue one right in front.

"I've had enough of you," the Maestro growled.

"Look out!" Lorelei cried.

But once again, she was too far away to help. All she could do was watch in horror as the Maestro aimed his baton. Its sickly light caught the blue citrustack as he yelped in panic.

"Noooo!" Lorelei cried, as the Maestro flicked his wrist, sending the citrustack flying off the back of the stage—and over the cliff beyond.

"You monster!" Lorelei shouted, tears half blinding her as she raced to the edge of the stage. Citrustacks were bouncy creatures. But even a citrustack couldn't possibly survive a fall from that height.

She felt a horse gallop past her so fast, she could hardly tell what it was. When the horse slowed down, Lorelei saw that it was Dart. He spread his wings as he neared the edge of the stage, and she guessed what he was about to do.

"Dart, no!" she yelled, flashing back to the colt's near-disastrous flight across a different—and much smaller—river. But Dart ignored her. Reaching the edge, he flung himself into midair, his wings flapping for all they were worth.

Harmony let out an anxious whinny as Dart plunged down out of sight. Lorelei raced to the edge, holding her breath. When she looked down, she saw that Dart's wings were now folded against his back as he plummeted after the citrustack.

"He's got him!" Lorelei shouted, as she saw the colt catch the fuzzy blue creature in his teeth and toss him back onto his withers.

Finally, Dart started pumping his wings. The citrustack clung to his back, his frightened whoops drifting up to the watchers. Once again, Lorelei held her breath. Could Dart do it?

For a second, he couldn't. He kept falling, getting closer to the jagged rocks of the riverbed.

But then his descent slowed . . . and he started to rise!

"Dart!" shouted Lorelei. "You're doing it! You're flying!"

She turned and hugged Harmony, pressing her tear-streaked face into her glossy coat. Harmony nickered happily. Moonsprite raced over to join in the celebration.

"Very nice." The Maestro's voice chilled Lorelei to her core. "But let's get back to the show, shall we?"

Spinning around, Lorelei saw that he was once again pointing his baton straight at her. Harmony saw it, too. She leaped in front of Lorelei.

"Stop!" Lorelei cried. "Don't try to protect me. I'd rather be his prisoner again than let him capture you as well."

The Maestro grinned. "Ah, but why choose?" he said. "I can arrange both!"

Thwack!

Something hit him from behind, knocking him to the ground. It was Dart! He'd flown all the way back up to the stage—just in time to come to the rescue again!

Lorelei lunged forward. The Maestro had lost his grip on the baton, and it was now skidding across the stage toward the drop-off. She had to get it, or her sister might be trapped forever!

She cried out in triumph as her hand closed over the smooth wood of the baton. When she sat up, the Maestro was back on his feet glaring at her.

"Now, now," he said through gritted teeth. "Let's not do anything stupid. Think of the music. The music! Didn't we make beautiful music together?"

"We don't need you to make music," Lorelei retorted. "You never had anything to do with it, anyway. You just stole the music from the rest of us!"

The audience gasped. The Maestro's face twisted with rage. "She's wrong," he shouted. "I'm the Maestro! I *am* music!"

"Really?" Glancing over, Lorelei saw that the citrustacks had just bounced the music box back onto the stage. It was a little dented, but still in one piece, its ornate lid flopped open. "In that case, I know the perfect place for you!"

She aimed and fired, sending a sizzle of magic light out of the tip of the baton. "Noooo!" the Maestro wailed, as the light enveloped him, shrinking him down.

Lorelei didn't hesitate. With a flick of her wrist, she flung him into the music box.

But she still wasn't finished. Aiming the baton at the box, she zapped the rest of its inhabitants back out. First, Bongo. Then the old violinist and the harp seal. And finally, Serena.

"Lorelei!" the little girl cried, racing over and flinging her arms around her. "I knew you'd come back for us!"

Lorelei hugged her tightly. "I'd never leave you," she said. "And guess what? We never have to go back in that horrible box!" She smiled around at the others. "None of us."

The old violinist shot an anxious look

at the music box. "But what if he gets out?" he quavered, clutching his violin to his chest. "He'll be so angry. . . ."

"He won't get out if Mr. Smithin the blacksmith has anything to do with it," said a voice from behind Lorelei. She looked behind her and saw the bearded man they had met earlier in the evening.

"Do you think he can make a lock for us?" Lorelei asked hopefully.

The bearded man chuckled. "Better yet, he could weld the box shut forever, if that were your wish."

Lorelei sighed in relief. She jumped, startled, when the audience erupted into applause.

"They still think it's part of the show!" Serena whispered in wonder.

"Must be the last effects of the Maestro's magic." Lorelei shrugged and glanced from her sister to Harmony to the others. "What do you think? Should we play the finale?"

Serena nodded. Harmony's eyes

sparkled. The lyre's strings riffled at a playful level. Bongo chattered and smacked his tail on the boards. Moonsprite began to dance, and Dart leaped into the air and flew overhead. The violin player and the harp seal joined in. The citrustacks bounced in time with the music.

Lorelei laughed out loud. She couldn't remember the last time she'd been so happy. Her mouth opened, and she sang out with pure joy.

A second passed before she realized she was singing the song she'd sung with the foals when they'd first met:

The lyrics seem to come to me,
Just like a distant memory . . .

They'd barely finished the first verse when they heard the loud trumpet of a stallion from somewhere in the audience. Dart's eyes opened wide, and he called back, nearly crashing to the stage. The crowd parted as half a dozen adult horses raced toward the performers.

"What's happening?" Serena cried, clutching at Lorelei.

"Don't worry," Lorelei said, her smile stretching from ear to ear as she recognized the horses. "It's the foals' parents. They heard the song and found us!"

She watched as the foals leaped off the stage, joyfully greeting their parents. For a second they were lost to view as the crowd shifted, and she felt a pang of sadness. Her friends were back with their families. But what would happen to her and Serena, who had no family?

It doesn't matter, she thought, reaching over to hug her sister. *We'll be together—and free. That's all that's important.*

When the crowd shifted again, she noticed an older woman with silver hair and thin glasses had joined the group of horses. She was speaking to them intently. All the while, she kept glancing over at the girls.

"Who's that?" Serena asked.

Lorelei shrugged. "I've never seen her before," she said. "But come on, we should go say good-bye to Harmony and the others. With the crowd at this festival, we could lose track of them easily."

She felt another pang. After their rocky start, she and Harmony had grown close—closer than Lorelei would have believed possible. What would become of their friendship now?

As she approached, the silver-haired woman turned and smiled at her. "Ah, Lorelei and Serena," she said in a rich, cultured voice. "I'm Mrs. Ronata. Harmony has just been telling me about you. Is it true you have no family—nowhere to go?"

Lorelei nodded, suddenly afraid to speak. Tears came to her eyes as she realized just how alone she and her sister were in the world.

Mrs. Ronata reached out and touched her cheek with a gentle hand. "I'm happy to say that's no longer the case. You see, I'm headmistress at the Polyphony Academy of

Music. I'd like you both to come and live there. It will be hard work, and you'll have much to study. But I think you'll find it as rewarding as I have."

"Really?" Serena asked. "You mean, music school?"

Lorelei's heart soared. "Oh, thank you, Mrs. Ronata. Thank you so much!"

"After the way you two sang tonight, the pleasure is all mine." Mrs. Ronata chuckled. "And don't worry, I know going to a new school is sometimes difficult. But you two will already have a friend there."

"Really? Who?" Lorelei asked.

The headmistress pointed to Harmony. "Harmony and her family live nearby. She plays her lyre with us all the time."

Lorelei couldn't contain her happiness. She raced over and hugged the violet filly. Harmony wrapped her neck around her, nuzzling her back as her lyre played several joyful chords. The citrustacks poured down off the stage, bouncing into Serena's arms as she giggled happily.

Tears of joy streamed down Lorelei's cheeks. She did the only thing she could think of to express what she was feeling— she sang, her voice blending with the clear notes of the lyre.

And you will be my Harmony;
Yes, you will be my Harmony!

he stallion strode into full view,
standing tall and splendid in the
yard. His blue-gray speckled coat and flowing black mane were even more striking than
they had seemed in Jillian's dream.

"Oh, he's gorgeous," Jillian breathed.
Smiling at the young stallion, she put her
hand on Conall's neck, curling her fingers
into his thick ruff.

But then Jillian got a look at the
roan's expression—his ears were laid back
flat against his head, and he danced on all

fours as if the ground were burning his hooves. His eyes rolled and Jillian could see white around the rims.

"He seems upset," Conall commented.

At the sound of the wolf's voice, the roan shied, dancing sideways. Conall's neck ruff bristled, and he let out a low growl.

"It's all right," Jillian said, trying to calm them both. She held out a hand tentatively toward the horse. "No one's going to hurt you. What's your name?"

The stallion whinnied, and a dull gray cloud wisped like faint smoke off his body. The cloud expanded, floating toward Conall and Jillian.

"What is that?" Jillian cried in alarm.

"Get back," Conall growled, and leaped protectively in front of Jillian. He snarled a challenge to the horse.

This meeting was not going well at all!

Go to
www.bellasara.com
and enter the webcode below.
Enjoy!

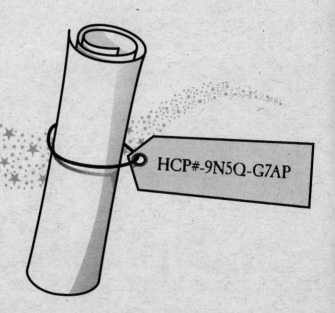

HCP#-9N5Q-G7AP